For Indeera – J.G.
Welcome Lalit – N.M.

Text copyright © Jamila Gavin 2002
Illustrations copyright © Nilesh Mistry 2002
Book copyright © Hodder Wayland 2002

Consultant: Joniah Parthasarathi
Editor: Katie Orchard

Published in Great Britain in 2002
by Hodder Wayland, an imprint of
Hodder Children's Books.

Cataloguing in Publication Data
Gavin, Jamila
Coming Home: A story about Divali. – (Celebration stories)
1. Divali – Juvenile fiction 2.Children's stories
I. Title
823.9'14 [J]

ISBN: 0 7502 3659 0

Printed in Hong Kong by Wing King Tong.

Hodder Children's Books
A division of Hodder Headline Limited
338 Euston Road, London NW1 3BH

CELEBRATION STORIES

Coming Home

JAMILA GAVIN

Illustrated by Nilesh Mistry

HODDER
Wayland

an imprint of Hodder Children's Books

 # Celebrating Divali

The word 'Deepawali', more popularly known as 'Divali', means 'a cluster of light' in Sanskrit – the ancient language of India. Divali is celebrated as a festival of light. It is a symbol of the triumph of light over darkness, and it pays tribute to Lakshmi, the goddess of wealth and prosperity.

Divali is celebrated in the Hindu month of *Kartika*, and, depending on the cycle of the moon, can happen either in October or November.

All over the Hindu world people clean their households and buy new clothes for this special time. The clerks get new ledger books and debts are cleared. Crops have been harvested. It is seen as the time for a new beginning.

Divali is celebrated in many different ways in different parts of India. In the north, it is linked to the famous story of Rama and Sita, and celebrates Rama's victory over the demon king, Ravana, and the rescue of Sita from his clutches.

When Rama and Sita returned to Ayodhya, the capital city of the kingdom of Khosala, after fourteen years in exile, people lit lamps and strung garlands all over their houses to welcome them home. Rama is an Avatar, an incarnation of the god, Lord Vishnu. Sita is also an Avatar, an incarnation of Lord Vishnu's wife, the goddess Lakshmi.

To welcome the goddess Lakshmi into their homes, Hindus make beautiful rangoli patterns out of coloured powders, rice and flour in the thresholds of their doorways, and they light oil lamps and fairy lights all over their houses and neighbourhoods. Everywhere, it is a time for feasts and parties.

A Time for Waiting

It was autumn. The leaves had fallen from the trees. The days were long and dark, and winter was coming. The wind moaned. Clouds raced by in the sky like galloping wild horses with streaming tails. A stripy cat crept along the wall like a tiger.

Dad pointed at the moon. It was full and gleamed like a silver coin. "How bright the moon is," he said. "When it becomes a new moon and gives hardly any light, we will celebrate Divali, and have a party."

"Oh, good!" cried Arjun, Suresh and Preeta. "We'll get new clothes!"

There was joy and happiness in the city of Ayodhya. The old king had decided to give up the throne in favour of Prince Rama, whom everyone loved.

"Look how the time has gone!" cried Mum. "It will be Divali before we know it. I must clean the house."

All the floors had to be polished, all the carpets cleaned, all the ornaments dusted. Every single plate, cup, saucer, spoon, knife and fork had to be washed, and every single saucepan, dish  and frying pan had to be scoured. The house had to be sparkling, because the goddess Lakshmi would come to visit at Divali.

Grandma said, "I must start to make sweetmeats for the party." She hunted in her cupboards for coconut, sweet rice, semolina, pastry flour, cardamoms, almonds, cloves and honey.

But the joy turned to sorrow. Instead of celebrations for a coronation, there was weeping and wailing. Prince Rama should have been crowned king, but something terrible had happened. Rama's stepmother remembered that the old king had promised her two wishes, because she had once saved his life. Now she wanted her wishes.

"My first wish," she declared, *"is that my son, Bharata, is crowned king instead of Rama. My second wish is that Rama is banished to the jungle for fourteen years."*
Everyone was horrified, especially when Rama's wife, the princess Sita, said she would go with him. They would both surely die.

Then Rama's younger brother, Lakshmana,
said that he would share their exile.
"With me by their side," said Lakshmana, "they
may have a chance of surviving the perils of
the jungle."
"Please come back," said Bharata, who didn't want
to be king. "I will never wear the king's slippers,
nor sit on the throne, and I will try
and rule wisely till you return."

So Rama, Sita and Lakshmana set off. They found
a clearing in the forest and built a little hut in it.
They hoped to live there until their exile was over.

*Sita lit a fire; its sacred flames would cook their
meals by day, and give them light in the fearful
darkness of the night.*
*Rama and Lakshmana sharpened their arrows.
They were all hungry, so the men were
going hunting.*
*"Watch out for tigers and leopards, and for
crocodiles and snakes," cried Sita anxiously.
"And don't forget – there are demons in
the jungle, too!"*

The cat stopped, one paw raised, still as a statue. Still as a hunter seeing its prey. Eyes glinted in the grass. A tail flicked.

The moon was half full.

A monstrous creature, a demon princess, watched
Prince Rama. She wanted him for her husband, so
she transformed herself into a beautiful woman.
"Rama, Rama, come with me and be my husband,
and I will give you all the powers of the universe."
But Rama said, "Go away, temptress. I don't want
your powers – and I don't want you. I already
have a wife whom I love."
The demon princess was furious. She tried to
tempt his brother, Lakshmana.

*"Lakshmana, Lakshmana! Come with me and
be my husband, and I will give you all the powers
of the universe."*

*But Lakshmana turned her away angrily.
The jealous demon princess leapt at Sita like a wild
cat and tried to claw out her eyes, but Lakshmana
took his sword and swiped off her nose.
"AAAAaaaaaH!" shrieked the monstrous princess,
and she rushed back to her brother.
Her brother was no ordinary brother. He was
Ravana, the ten-headed demon king.
"Look what they've done to me! I want revenge!"
screamed the demon princess.*

New Clothes

A cat stared through the grass. The lights from a passing car reflected in his eyes and turned them to gold.

"Come on, you three! It's Divali, and I'm going to town to buy new clothes," said Dad. "You can come, too. We must all have new clothes for Divali."

Arjun, Suresh and Preeta went into town with their father. The shops were bright and full of good things to buy. They went from window to window, looking at all the clothes. There was so much: stripy shirts, jazzy shirts, colourful Hawaiian shirts, and smart, crisp white shirts; baggy trousers, flared trousers, zipped-up trousers, sporty trousers, and smart, creased pin-striped trousers; frilly dresses, cotton dresses, silken dresses, satin dresses with ribbons and bows, and gold-threaded salwar kameez.

They went into the department store. It was very big. Lifts buzzed up and down, and escalators glided from floor to floor, carrying hundreds of people.

"Don't get lost," warned Dad, as they spread out looking at everything.

Sita wandered into the forest to collect herbs for her cooking pot. Suddenly, she saw a deer, a tame one that didn't run away. It was the most beautiful creature she had ever seen, with jewelled horns and a golden coat of fur.

Sita went rushing back to the hut.

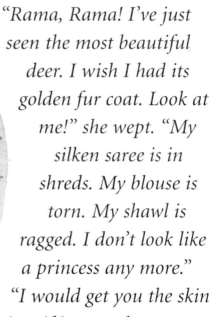

"Rama, Rama! I've just seen the most beautiful deer. I wish I had its golden fur coat. Look at me!" she wept. "My silken saree is in shreds. My blouse is torn. My shawl is ragged. I don't look like a princess any more."

"I would get you the skin of a tiger if it was what you wanted," cried Rama. He picked up his bow and arrows. "I'll go and hunt the deer."

"No, don't go!" warned Lakshmana. "The jungle is full of demons. It could be a trick."

But Rama went anyway.

Pink Shirt, Purple Pants

Dad bought himself a white shirt, a bright green tie and a brown jacket and trousers, and then Arjun and Suresh rushed off to look at trousers and shirts for boys.

"I want these trousers!" said Arjun. They were purple. He tried them on. "And I like this shirt." It was pink. He pulled it on, too.

"These are the clothes *I* want for Divali," said Arjun firmly.

"You can't wear a pink shirt with purple trousers, can you?" frowned Dad.

But Arjun said, "I *like* wearing a pink shirt with purple trousers."

Dad shrugged doubtfully. "What will your mother say?" But he bought them anyway.

"Pink shirt, purple pants!" chanted Suresh at his brother. Then Suresh looked for clothes he liked.

He saw some green-and-blue stripy trousers. "I like these ones!" he cried.

"Ugh!" snorted Arjun.

"They're a bit bright," suggested Dad, nervously.

"And I like this!" Suresh held up a bright yellow shirt. "These are the clothes *I* want for Divali!"

"Sunflower, April shower!" chanted Arjun.

Dad shrugged again and said, "I don't know what your mother will say," but he bought them anyway.

"Where's Preeta?" Suresh said.

Dad and the boys looked around. Where *was* Preeta?

She wasn't with the dresses, or the skirts, or the shoes; she wasn't with the underwear or nightclothes.

She wasn't in the perfume and cosmetics section, or with the toys or the electrical items…

"Have you seen Preeta?" they asked everyone.

Lakshmana and Sita waited for Rama to return home. But he didn't come. The forest grew dark. The animals were strangely quiet. Suddenly, they heard Rama shouting, "Help me! Help me!" He sounded terrified.

Lakshmana grabbed his bow and arrows. He rushed from the hut to help his brother. But then he stopped. He didn't want to leave Sita alone. "Lakshmana! Save my husband. Save Rama," wept Sita.
But how could he save Rama and keep his promise to stay with Sita?

Lakshmana drew a circle round the hut. "Sita," he warned, "do not step outside this circle. As long as you stay inside the circle you will be safe from harm." Then he rushed off to look for Rama.

Sita was alone. She waited and waited. But Rama didn't come back, and neither did Lakshmana.
She was so afraid.
Then she saw someone. She rubbed her eyes. Could it be true? An old holy man was hobbling towards her. She rushed to get some food for his empty bowl. Trusting the holy man, she stepped outside the circle.
But it was a trick...

27

 # Lost in the Jungle

The cat gave a shriek and sprang into the air.
It fled over the wall, between the dustbins, and
disappeared down the dark alleyways of the city.

Lakshmana searched and searched for his brother.
At last, he saw him. "Rama! I've found you!"
But Rama said he hadn't been lost at all. It wasn't
his voice calling for help – he had been trying to
catch the deer, but it kept disappearing.
Then they knew they had been tricked.
They rushed back to the hut, but Sita had gone.

Preeta was lost.

She moved among the racks of clothes. It was like a jungle. She ran up and down between the coats and jackets, the blouses and waistcoats, but she couldn't find her father and brothers.

She saw an escalator going down. Down she went. More racks of clothes. She saw a lift and went inside. She pressed the button for the third floor.

Up she went, and arrived at the music and electrical goods section. It was full of CD players and radios and mobile phones and wide-screen television sets and every possible type of computer.

"Oh, no!" she cried. "Where's my dad? Where are my brothers?" She ran here and there, and finally fell into a heap among the flickering television screens and began to cry.

Rama and Lakshmana searched everywhere for Sita. They came across the old king of the birds. He was dying because he had tried to save Sita. "Save her? From whom? Where has she been taken?" cried Rama.

"They went s… s… south," gasped the bird, and died.

Rama and Lakshmana went south, too, travelling for days and weeks through the thick, dark jungle. One day, they arrived at the kingdom of the monkeys. They met Hanuman, the Monkey God.

"We've lost Sita. She's been kidnapped, but we don't know by whom, and where she has been taken," they wept in despair.

But Hanuman had special powers. He could fly like the wind, or be as invisible as air. He said, "I'll go and find Sita."
Hanuman flew over to the island of Lanka where the evil ten-headed demon king, Ravana, lived.
Perhaps Ravana had kidnapped Sita.
Hanuman searched everywhere – and then he found her. There was Sita, sobbing under a tree.

To the Rescue

"Hi! Is that my little cousin, Preeta?"

Preeta looked up. There stood her long, gangly grown-up cousin, Ravi.

Preeta cried even louder, but this time with relief. She had been found.

"We came shopping to buy Divali clothes," she gulped. "And I lost the others and I haven't found any new clothes, either."

33

Ravi got out his mobile phone. "I'll just call home and say I've found you, and then we can go and buy your clothes."

Preeta was so happy. Now she would have her new clothes for Divali!

"What did you want to buy?" asked Ravi.

"I wanted a satin blue party dress and a new pair of silver trainers," smiled Preeta.

"Will trainers go with your party dress?" asked Ravi looking puzzled. But he bought them for her anyway.

Hundreds and thousands of demons rushed out.
They captured Hanuman. They wanted to kill him.
But Ravana, the king of the demons said, "No! We
won't kill him, we will just make him look a fool."
So Ravana took a fiery brand, and set fire to the
monkey's beautiful long tail.

But Hanuman used his magic powers. He made
himself small, and slipped out of his chains. Then
with his fiery tail, he danced over the city of
demons and set it alight.

*Laughing, he sucked his tail to quench the flames
and flew back to Prince Rama. They got together
an army of monkeys and bears.*

"How will we cross the ocean?" cried Rama.
"We'll build a bridge of course!" said Hanuman.
*Everyone helped. They chopped down trees and
collected boulders, and soon a bridge stretched out
over the waves towards the island of Lanka.*

Then Rama led the monkey army across the bridge into battle. Ravana, the demon king, was waiting with his army of demons. His ten heads rolled and his twenty eyes burned.
"You'll never conquer me!" he cried.

 # The Golden Arrow

There was hardly any moon. Two cats faced each other in the gloom, their green eyes blazing with hatred. They were enemies. Their fur was stiff with rage, their claws tiger-sharp. They crouched low, ready to attack, and crept closer to each other, step by step.

The stripy tiger cat moved first. With a terrible yowl, he pounced. The ginger cat sprang into the air. Fur flew, claws scratched. The night rang with the cries of battle as the cats fought as if to the death.

There was a fierce battle. It went on and on and on. Every time Rama shot an arrow at one of Ravana's ten heads, another grew in its place. But Rama had one special arrow. It was the Golden Arrow of Brahma, and he could only use it if all else was lost. That moment was now. Rama fitted the golden arrow to his bow and fired.

It struck the demon in the heart. With a cry like a howling tornado, Ravana fell down dead. Good had triumphed over Evil, and everybody danced and sang.

Preeta and Ravi set off home.

It was very dark. The moon was like the edge of a silver coin. The shops and houses flickered with strings of coloured lights. Fireworks sprayed up into the night sky. Everywhere people lit their Divali lamps. Preeta and Ravi easily found their way back home. They could hear singing and dancing, and laughter and fun. The parties were in full swing.

When they got to Preeta's house, they carefully stepped over the wonderful rangoli pattern that Mum had made at the gate by sprinkling rice flour and coloured powders.

How relieved everyone was that Preeta had come home safe and sound. Dad was cross and happy, furious and laughing all at the same time.

When the hullabaloo died down, Mum said, "And what new clothes did you and Ravi buy for Divali?"

"I'll go and put them on," said Preeta, running upstairs to her room.

When it was clear that Ravana, the king of the demons, was dead, Hanuman went and found Sita. He led her before Prince Rama.
The whole universe rejoiced, because Prince Rama was really the lord god, Vishnu, Preserver of the Universe, and Sita was his consort, the goddess Lakshmi, the Bringer of Wealth and Good Fortune.

The party guests began to arrive.

"Where are you, children?" called Mum. "Come down and join the party! Let everyone see your new clothes."

Down came Arjun in his pink shirt and purple trousers. Down came Suresh in his green stripy trousers and bright yellow shirt. Down came Preeta in her white and blue frilly party dress and her brand-new silver trainers.

"Good heavens!" cried Mum.

Everyone gasped.

Grandma threw up her hands in horror. "What *have* you all got on?" she exclaimed.

"It's what they wanted," shrugged Dad.

"It's what she wanted," shrugged Ravi.

"That's the last time you go Divali shopping without me!" laughed Mum.

But they all enjoyed the party anyway – especially Ravi, who loved Grandma's sweetmeats.

Prince Bharata was waiting when Rama, Sita and Lakshmana returned home after fourteen years in the wilderness. "At last, Rama, you can wear the king's slippers," he said joyfully, "and sit on your rightful throne."

When the party was over and everyone was asleep in bed, another visitor came. A strange and wondrous Being swept over the rangoli pattern on the path, paused, smiled, and entered the house.

It was Sita, the goddess Lakshmi. That night, she visited every house which was clean and sparkling and had celebrated Divali, and showered blessings on them.

 # *Glossary*

Avatar A divine or holy incarnation.

Ayodhya The capital city of the kingdom of Khosala.

Exile To be banished from one's home or country.

Incarnation To be born again as the same soul but in another time or likeness.

Rangoli pattern A decorative pattern, made by sprinkling coloured powders or grains.

Sanskrit An ancient holy language of Hindus, which is still in use.

Salwar kameez Indian dress found mainly in the north. It is made up of a long tunic and loose trousers. A veil, known as a *dupatta,* is often worn round the shoulders as well.

CELEBRATION STORIES

Look out for these other titles in the **Celebration Stories** series:

The Best Prize of All by Saviour Pirotta
Linda has spent months growing a giant pumpkin for the
Harvest Festival. She knows she's going to win the prize for the
biggest vegetable. But she's not the only one who wants first
prize. So when Linda's pumpkin is stolen the night before the
competition, she's convinced she knows who's responsible…

The Guru's Family by Pratima Mitchell
When Baljit visits the Panjab, he realizes that his family is
scattered around the world – just like the stars in the night sky.
So, when Guru Nanak's Birthday comes, Baljit and his cousin,
Priti, use the Internet to bring everyone together.

The Taste of Winter by Adèle Geras
Naomi is going to talk about Hanukkah at her school's Winter
Festivals Assembly. She needs something for the display – but
what? Just when she thinks she's found the answer, a perfect
solution comes from an unexpected place.

You can buy all these books from your local bookseller, or order them direct
from the publisher. For more information about Celebration Stories, write
to: *The Sales Department, Hodder Children's Books, a division of Hodder
Headline Limited, 338 Euston Road, London NW1 3BH.*